Hanapepe, Kauai
Hawaii 6-94

Tales from a Small Round Island

by

Joy Jobson

Illustrations by Jean Inaba

Elliott & Fitzpatrick, Inc.

Elliott & Fitzpatrick, Inc.
P.O. Box 1945
Athens, GA 30603
1-706-548-8161

Book design by Dawn Fraser
Cover painting by Jean Inaba

Library of Congress Cataloging

Jobson, Joy
Tales from a Small Round Island
1. Jobson, Joy   2. Island Legends
Fiction I. title
ISBN #0-945019-33-5

For Adam, Christy, Brian, Brooke, Neil, Laura, Kira,
Nicholas, Joshua, Cassady, Jorma, Christopher, Aysha
and Ryan "Bear"

ACKNOWLEDGEMENTS

I wish to acknowledge and thank Dawn Fraser whose initial idea and dream it was to publish these tales, and whose labor and skill brought together the stories and art to create the design of this book.

My thanks also go to Irma Fairall who so generously commissioned the art, which gave it beauty.

And my appreciation and thanks to Tim Field who made our dream come true by publishing this book.

CONTENTS

	Introduction	ix
I	Dolphin Child	1
II	White Flower	13
III	The Chameleon	27
IV	The Cloud Catchers	33
V	The Hibiscus	45
VI	Sleeping Giant	53
VII	In the Belly of the Whale	63
VIII	The Rainbow	77
IX	The Fire Thrower	83
X	How the Earth Mother Came to the Small Round Island	95

INTRODUCTION

THE FIRST OF THESE TALES came to me as letters to my grandchildren on the mainland. I wanted to show them the place in which I lived and also fulfill some of the important duties of a grandparent, which I could no longer do in person. While a parent often has the thankless task of preparing a child for the world, which means the parent and child often will be at odds, the grandparent has the job of showing the child the timeless world that lies beyond the everyday, the world of magic and myth. I found in the beauty of Kauai a way to share that timeless, unbound world with my grandchildren.

Each tale started for me as a curiosity about a feature of the landscape or a "critter" on the island. As a child I often made up stories about my surroundings, and these tales came in much the same way. Some came from legends already written or told about the island that I changed to produce a more personally satisfying ending, one that to me somehow fits better. It wasn't until a few of these stories were written that I became aware of how each also fits a particular grandchild. These tales are not meant to be legends of a specific place named Kauai, but of a timeless, mythical place—a small, round island in the middle of the sea.

Working in the psychology field, I have learned the value of fairy tales and myths in our lives. If you take a moment to think of your own favorite fairy tale or myth and then review how it fits the way your life has progressed, you also may be surprised at the correlation you'll find. A myth allows a child to solve a problem or answer a question about life before he or she has fully developed reasoning power.

All this explanation of the tales is actually an after-thought. The tales themselves came simply and easily; often they were written in one sitting. I will only add that they are meant to be read aloud and shared by adults with children.

Joy Jobson
Kauai, Hawaii,
1992

The fairy-tale hero proceeds for a time in isolation, as the modern child often feels isolated. The hero is helped by being in touch with primitive things—a tree, an animal, nature—as the child feels more in touch with those things than most adults do. The fate of these heroes convinces the child that, like them, he may feel outcast and abandoned in the world, groping in the dark, but, like them, in the course of his life he will be guided step by step, and given help when it is needed. Today, even more than in past times, the child needs the reassurance offered by the image of the isolated man who nevertheless is capable of achieving meaningful and rewarding relations with the world around him.

Bruno Bettelheim
The Uses of Enchantment
Alfred Knopf, Inc. 1976

The boy's dolphin parents appeared in a silver flash and whisked him away with them.

I

Dolphin Child

E HAD BARELY COME from his mother's belly when he first swam. On that fateful day he dozed peacefully upon his mother's lap as his father paddled their dug-out canoe swiftly through the water. Halfway across the bay a school of dolphins joined them and rode playfully in their bow wake. Without warning, two large dolphins rose up as if arching for air and, with a bang of their heads, tipped the canoe. The baby flew from his mother's lap into the water.

His mother grabbed for him, but too late. Her baby disappeared beneath the sea. Horror-stricken, his mother grasped the side of the boat and rocked it violently. When the child's father turned to warn his wife about tipping the canoe, he stopped short. He stared at her empty lap and then into the calm sea. First those crazy dolphins banged his canoe—dolphins were never so clumsy—and now his child was gone, without a bubble or a shadow in the clear sea to tell him where.

Without a word or a wasted movement, he dived into the sea and squinted through water-clouded eyes. But he could find neither baby nor dolphins. As he pushed up from the sea bottom, he wondered how he could tell his wife the sad news: their first-born son had been swallowed by the sea gods. But even before he broke the surface, he saw the shadow of his wife, pointing. He grabbed the edge of the canoe and, brushing the water from his eyes, gazed up at her laughing face. He wondered if she had gone mad with grief.

"Look! Look!" she laughed and cried in the same breath.

He ducked under the canoe and hoisted himself up on the other side. Squinting in the direction of her pointing finger, he saw in the distance their tiny baby boy swimming between two large dolphins. He grabbed his paddle and stroked swiftly toward the strange trio. On closer inspection he saw that their baby was holding tightly with his small hands to a fin of each of the dolphins. Still holding his paddle, he reached for his wife's hand and the two watched, their faces at first perplexed, and then, wreathed in smiles.

"It is a sign," said his wife. "I remember you told me the dolphins were gathered in the bay the night he was born. You said then it was a good sign that he was loved by the water spirits."

"Look! He swims by moving his feet as if he had a dolphin tail," the husband said, dropping his wife's hand and paddling behind the strange threesome. "And see how he laughs with them when we have yet to see his first smile. I do not know about this child."

"I do," his mother replied. "I have known from the first moment he moved within me that he bore a special spirit. O husband, just listen to the dolphins." The soft breeze wafted the clicks and high-pitched whistles of the dolphins to their ears. "They are singing his praises."

"Those are only meaningless dolphin noises," the father said. "I must find a way to get him back."

But before he could draw closer, the two dolphins turned and swam directly to the canoe. As they came alongside, they paused, and the child's mother reached down and scooped her tiny son into her arms.

At home with his parents in their thatched-roof hut after his great adventure, the baby seldom smiled and never cried. No matter where they laid him down, he turned his head toward the sea and, with a look of sadness, quietly listened. In desperation his mother took the child to the bay and swam with him out beyond the breakers. As she swam she heard the song of the dolphins. The baby heard them, too. He laughed and clapped his hands. In an instant he squirmed from her grasp and was scooped up by his dolphin parents.

Stories about the strange Dolphin Child spread across the small, round island in the middle of the sea. Villagers came from all over to see this odd child and watch him swim with the two big dolphins.

As the Dolphin Child grew from baby to boy, he spent as much of his waking life in the sea as on the land. Soon he was old enough to help his father catch the fish for their supper. From the first, the Dolphin Child spurned the net and spear his father offered. Instead, he dived from their canoe and brought up the fish in his hands. Then, while still holding the fish, he would float on his back and speak to it in the clicks and whistles of the dolphins. If the fish nodded its head, the boy would hand it to his father. But if the fish shook its head, the boy would let it swim away.

Sometimes his father grew impatient as one fish after another shook its head. Once or twice he even tried to grab the fish from his son. But the boy simply spun away from his father and let the fish jump free.

"Stop grumbling," the boy's mother would say when her husband complained of their child's strange ways. "We have never had such bounty. And when others are in need, he brings fish to them, too. We are blessed."

"Or cursed," his father mumbled.

Now it happened at that time that the old island chief died and his place of honor was taken by his nephew, a warrior of great renown.

"I declare a week of festivities," the new chief said. " We will invite all the great chiefs of the other islands. In homage to them and to me, tomorrow each family must bring me twenty fish for salting. All who disobey will be branded enemies and drowned."

"Twenty fish!"

"The sea will think we are greedy!"

"How will those who are old, with no children, bring twenty fish?"

"How can our bountiful sea replenish itself if we empty it of fish?"

The same complaints and questions were heard all over the island. A wise elder of the village came before the new chief." A good ruler does not make impossible demands on his people," the elder said.

"What do you know about ruling, old man?" said the new chief. "Ask that crazy Dolphin Child to help. He seems to be able to pull any fish he chooses out of the sea."

The islanders, led by the wise elder, appealed to the boy and he agreed to help. In the morning a great funnel of canoes followed the child as he swam out to sea, holding the fins of his dolphin parents. At first many of the fish he caught agreed to be part of the great feast, but then more and more refused, pleading that they had families to raise.

As the sun crept toward the sea, ten fish in a row refused to be caught. Finally, the weary boy hoisted himself aboard his father's canoe and immediately fell asleep. The canoes held only half the fish needed.

"Maybe the rest have been caught by those on shore pulling the nets," the father said. But when they reached shore, the nets were almost empty.

"This is not enough," the new chief said, "I would be ashamed to share such meager fare with those coming from the far islands. Get me more!"

"It is only because of this blessed child we have even this many," the wise elder said. "We will complete your feast with fruits and wild boar."

"No! I must have more fish to salt," the chief insisted. "I know there are more than this in the sea. Send the boy for them. I hear he can catch as many fish as he chooses."

"It is true that there are more fish in the sea and that the Dolphin Child can catch all he chooses, but the boy only takes those that are willing to become food for us," the wise man said.

"What?" shouted the chief. "I will take that boy out in my canoe and there will be no foolishness about fish choosing to be caught or not!"

"I would not do that if I were you," warned the wise, old man. "This child is blessed with a special spirit."

The new chief waved his powerful arms and shouted, "I do not believe in such foolishness! I believe in a sun that warms me when I am cold, stars that guide my canoes into battle, and water that falls from mountains to quench my thirst. The fruit grows on trees for me to eat. The fish swim in the sea for me to catch. And the pigs roam the mountains to fill my belly. All the rest is foolishness spouted by weak, old men trying to appear wise. Get out of my sight before I have your wrinkled carcass boiled in the cook pot." With that, the new chief stomped off to find the Dolphin Child.

"Come!" he commanded when he spotted the boy. Without another word, he scooped the child up under his arm and strode off with him to his canoe. The chief paddled out silently. At a good fishing spot, he tossed the boy overboard.

The frightened child clicked and whistled to the fish swimming by, but none would come. The new chief smacked him with the paddle.

"Get fish, you lazy boy."

But no fish came. The sun dropped to the water's edge and the chill of evening made the boy shiver. But the new chief would not let him back in the boat.

Raising his paddle in anger, the chief shouted, " If you will not catch me fish, I will make you into food for them." But before he could strike, the boy's dolphin parents appeared in a silver flash and whisked him away with them.

The next day the new chief declared that all who had failed to bring their quota of fish must gather at the high ridge that formed a long tongue of land that stretched out above the ocean. All the island people gathered there instead of just the sick and old ones who were unable to fish. The chief cursed them for mocking him and dismissed all but the elderly.

"You are old and useless," the chief told them. "And anyone who cannot serve me cannot live on my island. Since you honor the Dolphin Child instead of me, you shall live with him in the sea. Let us see what protection he offers you now." His warriors stood each old person in a row facing the sea along the rim of the cliff.

"Go on, call on your spirits!" mocked the chief. The old ones remained silent. With a sneer the chief grabbed his paddle and, walking behind them, struck each in the middle of the back, shoving one after the other off the cliff.

Meanwhile the other islanders had paddled out to the open sea to wait, hoping they might rescue any of the old people who were not harmed by the fall and could float that far. But they need not have worried, for right below the cliff overhang, out of sight, hundreds of dolphins and the Dolphin Child waited.

As the old ones fell, a dolphin caught each one. The boy told them to take a deep breath and pray to the spirits to help them hold on. Then the dolphins swam into the ocean depths with their precious cargo, coming up where the villagers waited. By the time the dolphins surfaced, they were beyond the reach of the warriors' spears. All were saved.

"So they think they can defy me, " the chief said, glaring at the strange procession of old people and dolphins. "We'll see about that. Gather all my warriors and our largest canoes. I'll drown the lot of them."

On his way to the canoes, the wise old man, holding fast to his dolphin rescuer, heard clicks and squeals louder than any he had ever heard before from the dolphins, despite the fact that he was growing deaf. "What is happening?" asked this elder of the boy.

"A great wave is coming," the boy answered. "The dolphins say that we must stay far out in the sea where it will roll in, still flat before it crests, and cannot harm us."

As the old folks were pulled into the canoes by the villagers, the wise old man and the boy spread the word of the great wave. In terror the islanders turned their canoes out into the ocean. The dolphins sped along beside them and the force of their wake made the canoes fly over the waves.

Back on the beach, the chief ordered his great, ocean-voyaging canoes to be placed in the water. "All right, men. Push out!" he shouted. But just as they pushed the canoes into the ocean, the water receded, leaving their canoes high and dry.

"The spirits are warning us," the warriors whispered. "Trying to kill the old ones has angered them."

"You are cowards, afraid of your own shadows," the chief yelled. "Pick up those canoes and get them in the water!"

The warriors lifted the canoes and carried them out into what had been the middle of the bay, but now was just a sea of sand. A strange sound, at once a hush and yet a roar, surrounded them, touching their spirits and filling them with dread. As they dropped their canoes into the water, the sea rose in front of them as if it were a mighty serpent rearing upon its coils. The giant wave swept them up, up, up, until it dashed them against the very cliff from which the old ones had been shoved.

Some of the warriors died right away. Others were swept out to the open ocean as the water receded. Then suddenly, as if changing its mind, the sea with a fierce roar swept back again toward land. The great, foaming surf hurled the warriors against the cliff, crumbling its edge into a pile of stones. When the sea again receded, where the edge had been there remained only a pile of rocks and mangled bodies. Water now rushed between this strange outcropping of stones and men and the new cliff edge. A dolphin swam swiftly through this new opening and sped back to the ocean.

When the dolphin reached the canoes, he told the boy that the tidal waves were gone, the warriors were killed, and it was safe to return. On the way home, the weary old ones slept peacefully as the islanders paddled their canoes and worried about how their homes had fared.

Imagine their surprise when they found no damage from the giant waves. The only change was that there was a strange pile of rocks and men where the edge of the cliff had stood. In gratitude the islanders lit a fire on top of the cliff to thank the dolphins for their help. And from that day on, they followed the Dolphin Child's example and asked permission when taking fish from the sea. And so it is to this day.

If you should visit that small, round island in the middle of the sea, you will find a light still burns on that cliff. And in the sea the stone burial place of the wicked chief and his warriors lies beaten on all sides by wild, white, angry surf. Slip into the water at the base of the cliff and listen. If you come with respect and humility, the dolphins may greet you with spins and arcs and tell you in whistles and clicks of the wondrous Dolphin Child. Ask and you, too, may be given the privilege of swimming with them, just as the Dolphin Child did so long ago.

"She closed her eyes and with great effort saw herself dancing at the festival. A smile trembled on her lips."

II

White Flower

ONG AGO ON A SMALL, ROUND ISLAND in the middle of the sea there lived a tiny girl with long black hair, nut brown skin and feet with wide-spread toes. The first few years of the child's life were happy. But then, while she was still small, her mother, who always smiled and made her laugh, died. And although her father loved her dearly, he spent weeks away on long sea voyages. As the time for him to sail again neared, he hastily remarried so his child would be cared for while he was away.

His new wife made the girl work hard and scolded her over the tiniest mistakes. And her new sisters, who were older, called her a baby and teased her about her toes that were spread so wide apart.

Often while her father was gone, she would go to a grassy meadow at the edge of the sea, lean her back against a large rock and weep for her mother. One day as she wept a white dove with wide wings swooped down and alighted upon the rock. He cocked his head and looked at her.

"Why do you weep, child?" he asked.

"Because my dear mother is gone," she said with a sob, "and I have nothing but my tears to remind me of her."

"Would your dear mother want to know you are so sad?" the bird asked.

The girl shook her head and more tears came. "My mother was happy. She always sang and wore a flower in her hair. She used to put a flower in my hair, too."

"Why are there no flowers in your hair now?" asked the bird.

"Because my new sisters and mother say the flowers on our trees must be traded for food and clothes."

"Wait here for me," the bird said, and with two mighty flaps of his wings, he rose aloft.

A few minutes later he returned with a twig. He laid the twig at the girl's feet and flew off again. When he returned this time, he was riding on the head of a pig. The pig stopped beside the rock, bowed his head to the girl and then with his hooves dug a hole in the earth. When the hole was deep enough the pig and the white dove planted the twig. As soon as they were finished the pig bowed again and was gone.

"Water this twig each day, and soon you will have flowers for your hair," the white dove said. "And the perfume from the blossoms will remind you of your sweet mother."

Each day the girl came faithfully to visit the tiny tree. And each day she watered it with the tears of her sadness.

Years passed and the twig grew and grew until it was a full-size tree. Hundreds of white flowers with yellow centers covered its branches. The white of the flowers reminded the girl of her mother's pure sweetness and the yellow of her mother's sunny laughter. Every day as the maiden crossed the meadow the perfume from its flowers wafted on the sea breezes to greet her.

The girl also grew. Each day when she visited the tree, she would pluck a flower for her hair to remind her to be as happy and sweet as her mother once was. The villagers called her the girl with the white flower, then as time passed, just White Flower. Soon even her family called her White Flower.

One day when her father had been gone on a voyage for a long time, the girl overheard her new mother and sisters talking excitedly about a betrothal festival for a young chief from the other side of the island.

"Who will he choose to be his wife," the one sister asked, pointing to the other, "her or me?"

"He won't choose either one of you if you don't hurry," their mother complained. "We have much work to finish before we can paddle to the other side of the island. We must make clothes enough for all three days of the festival. Where is that lazy White Flower?"

"I'm here, Mother," White Flower answered, coming out from the shadows. "What do you wish me to do?"

"You must gather all the broad leaves from the bushes so we can make new skirts, and we will need all the flowers from our trees so that we can make leis for each day of the festival."

"Can I go, too?" White Flower asked.

"You're too young. The chief's son does not want a baby," said one sister.

"Who would love someone with such silly spread toes?" said the other.

"You must stay home and tend the fire and feed the animals," said her new mother. "You are not quite ready to be a wife."

"My father would let me go if he were here, " said White Flower.

"Well, he's not here and you must stay home," her new mother said. "Now get busy."

All day long White Flower worked hard. The next morning bright and early the three ordered her to push their canoe into the water, and off they paddled. White Flower watched sadly until they were out of sight, then went to her Mother tree and wept.

"Why are you crying?" She looked up and saw the white dove sitting on one of the branches. She told him how she longed to go to the festival, and how her new mother and sisters had made her stay home and tend the fire and feed the animals.

"Now they have gone and I must stay here to work."

"Well, crying about it won't help," the white dove scolded. "If you really want something badly enough, you must see yourself already having it. If you see, hear, smell and feel it is so, it will be so."

She closed her eyes and with great effort saw herself dancing at the festival. She listened very hard. Soon she heard the drums beating. She took a deep, deep breath through her nose. Her mouth watered. She smelled the pig roasting. She stretched out her hands. The warmth of the fire pit scorched her palms. And since she could see, hear, smell and feel herself there, she thought surely, through some magic, she must be there. But when she opened her eyes, she still sat beside her mother tree. And before her now stood, lined up in a row, a frog, an owl, and the same pig who had helped plant her mother tree.

"You need someone to tend the fire. I will do it," said the frog. "I will feed it dead twigs and croak all night to keep it alive with my breath."

"And I will spread my wings above it so the night showers will not put it out," said the owl.

"And I will see that all the animals, including me, are fed," said the pig.

"That would be wonderful," said White Flower, "but how will I get there? The festival will be over by the time I walk to the other side."

"See, hear, smell and feel it so!" commanded the dove.

Again she closed her eyes and with all her might saw, heard, smelled and felt her way to the other side. She opened her eyes and ran to the water's edge where a dolphin jumped above a wave. He emitted a whistle and nodded to her before splashing down again into the water.

"The dolphin will take me," the girl cried, running to the sea. "But, wait," she said, suddenly turning, "what about clothes? I will be all wet when I arrive." She looked at the dove, then smiled. "I know, I will see, hear, smell and feel them when I get there." With that she dove into the surf and swam out to the dolphin.

She clasped his back fin firmly and off they went through the sea. Every once in a while the dolphin would arc out of the water, checking the shore for how far they had come. At those times White Flower would lie flat and encircle his neck with her arms. It was a marvelous ride.

When at last they spotted a place on the other side of the island where many canoes were beached, the dolphin swam toward shore. The girl gave him a last hug, then dove in front of a wave, which swiftly carried her in.

As soon as she reached the beach, she closed her eyes and saw, heard, smelled and felt her new clothes for the festival.

When she opened them again, birds of every description were flying toward her with seaweed, grass, flowers, broad leaves and soft bark from the trees. They fluttered around her, weaving in and out of one another as if dancing around a Maypole. Soon she had a bodice woven of silken seaweed and a skirt sewn of broad leaves and soft bark. Around her neck, wrists and ankles were rings of flowers. And last of all, the white dove arrived from the other side carrying in his beak a white flower with a yellow center from her mother tree. With great ceremony, the dove placed his blossom in her hair. When she twirled about, heavenly perfume caused the birds to swoon dizzily.

"Thank you. Thank you. Thank you, all!" White Flower cried, twirling gaily. Chattering and singing, the birds circled about her head, once more making sure her costume was perfect before flying off to their nests. When they were gone, White Flower turned and ran up the path that led from the beach to the festival, her way lit by a great fire which turned the night sky orange.

The dancing had already begun. She stood beside a palm tree, watching. She knew the chief's son immediately because he was by far the most handsome. He danced with power and grace.

The perfume of the mother tree flower drew the chief's son to look at her and when he did, he thought her the most beautiful maiden there. He came before her and asked if she would dine with him. As they passed her new mother and sisters, the three stared at her, but then shook their heads. It was impossible that this lovely woman child could be White Flower. All evening long White Flower and the chief's son danced, ate and sat together.

When the festival was over for the night, the chief's son asked, "Where is your home? I will walk you there."

"Oh no, it is much too far," White Flower whispered. "It is on the other side of the mountain."

"But where will you sleep tonight?" asked the chief's son. "Let me take you."

"I must swim there," said White Flower, "and I swim very fast. Only if you can swim as quickly can you come with me. If you cannot, I will see you tomorrow night."

"Surely you cannot swim as swiftly as I," said the chief's son. And with that they ran into the water.

White Flower dove under a wave where she knew she would find her dolphin friend. When she saw him, she grabbed onto his fin, and they were off for their voyage to the other side. The chief's son searched and searched, called and called, but she was gone. Sadly, he caught the next breaking wave and rode it to the shore.

All that night he worried. He could not believe the beautiful maiden could swim faster than he, so he assumed she had drowned.

The next evening as he sat moping at the festival, the perfume of the flower from the mother tree wafted past him. He jumped up. White Flower came into the clearing in her beautiful gown of seaweed, bark, leaves and flowers. His joy knew no bounds. Again they danced and sang and feasted. By now all were sure the beautiful maiden from the other side had won his heart.

Again that night when the evening's festivities were over, the two swam out to sea. This time the chief's son stayed very close to his beloved. He saw her grab the dolphin's fin and swim away with it. Swimming to shore, his heart was even heavier. What if she were a mermaid? Or from the underworld? Could she be his wife, give him children? He hardly slept.

The next evening before White Flower left for the third and final day of the festival, the dove warned her that she must return that night.

"But the chief's son is to pick a wife and marry her tonight," White Flower cried. "I know he will pick me. I can see, hear, smell and feel it is so."

"You must not marry him without your father's knowledge," the dove said.

"But. . .but. . ." Before she could say another word he was gone.

White Flower knew the dove was right. Her dear father must know. Because of her heavy heart, it was hard for her to close her eyes and imagine herself at the festival. Still, after great effort she managed to do it, and her dolphin arrived.

The chief's son met her at the beach. He asked her what kind of enchanted spell she was under and why she rode on the back of a dolphin. When White Flower would not answer, the chief's son said he did not care, that he would marry her anyway. Tears filled her eyes and crept over their rims, wending their way down her cheeks as White Flower slowly shook her head.

"I love you," the chief's son declared. "You must marry me tonight."

"I cannot," White Flower said sadly. "My father would be very unhappy if I married without his knowledge."

"But it is decreed that tonight I must marry," the chief's son said with alarm.

"I know," White Flower answered. "You must find someone else."

Later the chief's son danced each dance with a different maiden as White Flower sat on the edge of the clearing and tearfully watched. If only her father would come.

Suddenly she had an idea. What if she could see, hear, smell and feel her father come? She closed her eyes and saw his great sailing canoe with its paddles lying idle on the deck, she heard the whistle of the wind and the flapping of the sail, she smelled the salt in the sea air and the fresh-caught fish cooking for the sailors' supper. She touched her father's cheek and kissed him.

"Hurry home, father, please," she begged, taking his hand and kneeling before him. She heard him call to his men to paddle with the wind that he felt his daughter needed him. All evening as the chief's son danced, she sat with her eyes tightly closed, urging her father to come to her.

"White Flower," the chief's son called, startling her. "White Flower, wake up. I want one last dance with you before I choose my wife."

White Flower only kept her eyes more tightly closed. The chief's son walked away filled with sadness. The maidens at the festival all lined up in a row and he looked carefully at each one but his heart was not in it.

Then from the beach there came a great roar. The wind and tide drove a large canoe onto the sand to the cheers of the sailors. White Flower jumped up and raced to the beach. The chief's son raced after her. And what do you think they found?

Of course, it was her father. He jumped over the side of his canoe and grabbed little White Flower up in his arms, and kissed her many times before he placed her back on the sand.

"Father, father, I am so happy you came," she cried, still tightly holding his hand. "This is the chief's son, whom I wish to marry. Tonight is the last night of the betrothal festival and he must choose right now. He had chosen me, but I knew I could not accept him without your knowledge."

Her father, who had always shown great talent for picking good men for his voyages, knew in an instant that this man was the right one for his precious daughter. He took her hand still clasped in his and gave it to the chief's son.

On the edge of the crowd his new wife and daughters saw that the beautiful maiden was indeed their White Flower.

"She cannot marry the chief's son," the mother declared. "She disobeyed, and now when we go home our animals will be dead and the fire will be out."

"No," said White Flower. "The animals are alive and the fire is burning. I have been home every night to check."

"Even if that is so," said the oldest sister, "she is too young to marry."

"And she has ugly, spread toes," said the other.

"It is time for White Flower to marry," her father said. "I was sailing home and she came to me, as if in a dream, and told me she was ready. We even used our paddles to make the journey more swift. Come, let us be happy for her."

As the chief's son and White Flower stood before the priest to be married, the white dove and all the birds of the island flew overhead with flowers from her mother tree in their beaks. As the young couple kissed a shower of fragrant white blossoms with yellow centers rained down upon them and the others present.

And from that day forward, the two loved each other deeply and had many children, and their children gave them many grandchildren. For each new child and grandchild they planted a branch of the mother tree on a different part of the island. And if today you should find that small, round island in the middle of the sea, you most likely would be greeted with a kiss and a fragrant lei of white flowers with yellow centers such as the ones from the mother tree. And you might also note if you care to, that your greeter has feet with wide-spread toes, just like those of little White Flower.

"The lizard screamed, but no sound came . . . Hastily, he backed toward the sea. But just as he did so, the islanders raised their giant net."

III

The Chameleon

NCE UPON A TIME, before history books were written, the Goddess of Fire lived on a small island in the middle of the sea. Each day she worked mightily to make this island perfectly round. First she would spill lava down one side of the mountain, then she would pour it down the opposite side so that the island formed a perfect circle.

All went well until one day a giant lizard rose out of the sea and spouted water from his great mouth onto the lava that was burning its way down the slope. He shot so much sea water on the fiery lava, it came to a stop before it reached the ocean, creating a cliff. Annoyed, the Goddess of Fire threw more of her fiery lava down. But again he spouted water and stopped it. Everywhere she poured her lava the lizard stopped it before it reached the sea. The island lost its roundness.

Now this change in shape made the island people unhappy. The great cliffs created by the stopped lava blocked their way to the sea. When they scolded the giant lizard, he replied with rude, nasty words and stuck out his great black tongue.

Even the Goddess could do nothing with the nasty creature. For every time she threw her fire at him, he ducked into the sea where the Sea God welcomed and protected him. Now the Sea God and the Goddess of Fire had been enemies for a long time. Each was always trying to invade the kingdom of the other.

Furious at being tricked, the Goddess of Fire raged and ranted. Showers of fire rained on the people. Their homes were burned. The fruit dried on their trees. Their vegetables withered in blackened fields.

At least once every day the lizard would stick his head up out of the sea, shout rude words and stick his tongue out at the Goddess and the islanders.

"Please, help us get rid of this foul-mouthed beast," the people begged the Goddess. "Our island is losing its beauty and we do not have a moment's peace."

"If you can trap him on the beach," the Goddess said, "I will scorch his tongue from his mouth with my fire."

So one day, soon after, the islanders gathered on a beach that bordered a half-moon bay where the lizard often appeared. Each carried a fishing net. By the light of the moon they sewed their nets together. The next morning just as the sun peeked up over the sea, they laid the giant net in the shallow water, stretching it from one end of the bay to the other. Around the edges of the net, the people stood, waiting.

Up in her fiery pit, the Goddess waited, too.

Late that afternoon, just as they were about to give up for the day, the lizard's head popped up from the water. The islanders watched silently as the lizard crawled across the sea floor to the beach. The Goddess sent her fiery lava down the mountain. The lizard stopped it with a river of water, and then stuck out his tongue.

"If you're so clever," the Goddess said, "let's see you drown out my fire in the center of this mountain."

The giant lizard filled his mouth with water and eased his huge body halfway out of the sea. He shot water in a curve up to the top of the mountain. The Goddess' fire hissed and smoked. The lizard yelled something rude. Then he stuck his tongue out as far as he could. The Goddess threw a ball of fire at him which rolled down his tongue and into his throat. He screamed, but no sound came. For his tongue, which had been blackened by the fire, had fallen out onto the sand.

Hastily, he backed toward the sea. But just as he did so, the islanders raised their giant net. His legs and tail got entangled in the netting. He could not move. The fire raged in his throat as he thrashed about helplessly.

As the fire burned, the lizard began to shrink. He got smaller and smaller. Soon the villagers and the children lost their fear of the foul mouthed creature and moved closer to him. He shrank and shrank until he was no bigger than a hibiscus flower.

A small, tender-hearted boy, who stood watching with the other children, ran to the sea and scooped up a bowl full of water. Before anyone could stop him, he threw the water down the, by now, tiny lizard's throat, putting the fire out.

As the villagers laughed and scoffed at him, the lizard slithered away, shamed and humbled. Once again the people could launch their canoes and pick fruit from their trees. And the Goddess of Fire, happy the rude fellow had been dealt with, went back to creating her perfect island.

Now some would say that this tale is not true. But if you search hard, you will find this small round island—not perfectly round, of course, because of the lizard's mischief—where even to this day the creature's foul, black tongue can be seen at the edge of the sea on a beautiful beach. And if you sit very still and watch by a tree, a small chameleon lizard, just like the one shrunk by the Goddess, may happen by. If he spots you, he will puff out his throat, and then you will see, still caught in its center, the shadow of the Goddess's fire.

"And while those clouds clung to the rim of the sacred mountain, pouring rain down its sides to the valleys below, the four were released from their stone bonds to chant and dance and live happily together."

IV

The Cloud Catchers

ONG AGO AND FARAWAY when the great gods still stalked the small, round island in the middle of the sea, girl and boy twins were born to the royal family. The islanders rejoiced in their great, good fortune. For you see in those days on that island it was traditional for royal brothers and sisters to wed each other. Even the gods, pleased by this fortuitous birth, promised years of sunny skies, fruitful harvests and bountiful seas. The brother and sister twins grew up in a land of harmony and plenty.

Years before the twins were destined to marry, the islanders were planning the royal wedding. The twins accepted their fate, glad they would always be together.

But a short time before their sixteenth birthday, something changed. The boy twin on a lone hunting trip met a girl from the other side of the mountain and, as if enchanted, fell in love with her. From that day on the boy would sneak off early in the morning to the mountains to meet the girl. Often his sister asked where he was going, but he would not tell her. He did not know how to explain his sadness when he did not see the girl from the other side of the mountain.

At first the boy's twin missed him, but then later she found she, too, enjoyed having days by herself. On those days when her brother disappeared she would go to a waterfall that fell from the top of the great mountain. There she would swim and play in the pool at the base of the fall, and, afterward, sit beside it and sing while she dried her hair.

As she sang she would pretend a great chief from another island had fallen in love with her and wanted to marry her. She would answer his pleas of love and devotion with great, sad, love songs, which harmonized with the rush of water spilling down the fall into the river. Her songs floated upon the river and out to the ocean.

As love would have it, a young chief from a neighboring island did hear the girl twin's love songs. And one day he decided to paddle his canoe across the great waters to find the place and the one singing. The villagers of his island scoffed at his decision since all knew the water between the two islands was the home of the Sea God, with a channel so rough the boy's chances of survival were very slight.

The young chief's parents asked, "Why do you want to take such a great risk when you know you have responsibilities here?"

"You will think me mad if I tell you," the young chief said, bowing his head to hide his eyes.

"You have always been a sensible, obedient son," his mother said. "We know you are not mad. Tell us." The boy sighed. How could they understand?

"We worry that you are challenging the gods," his father said. "You must tell us what draws you to such a faraway place?"

"Father, you'll laugh," the boy said, digging his toes into the sand.

His father stood very tall and stern, but said nothing. The boy looked off across the sea toward the island that lay out of sight over the horizon and then in a soft voice said, "Sometimes when I sit here at the edge of the sand and the water is calm and the winds are still, I hear the singing of a woman. It comes from over there." He pointed to the horizon. "Her voice stays with me all day. It sings to me in my dreams at night. I have tried to ignore it, but I cannot. I must find the woman of that voice."

"This is the work of the gods," his mother whispered. "Only they could make a voice carry across the sea. Be careful, my son. The gods are jealous of handsome, young chiefs who hunt and fish as well as you do. They are trying to trick you into doing something foolish."

"Mother, the voice will not let me rest," the boy said. "I cannot fish. I cannot hunt. I am sick with longing."

His mother walked to the edge of the sea and stretched out her arms as if speaking to a crowd. "Leave my son be!" she wailed. "He is all I have. You have taken my other children, and now you want him, too."

The boy knelt before his mother. "No, mother, the voice I hear is kind and warm. It is the voice of the woman I love."

"It is a trick," his mother warned. "If it is not, why do your father and I not hear this voice? You must not listen!"

"No. He must listen," the chief said quietly, "He is a man now and must follow the voice he hears. Son, we will prepare a sturdy canoe that will withstand the high waves of the channel."

The next day the chief sent his son and the strongest men of the village into the mountains to find just the right tree for the canoe. They searched and searched, but by nightfall they still had not found the tree they sought. Tired, they lay down upon the soft, long, ironwood needles and slept.

In his sleep that night the chief's son heard the beautiful voice. In the purest of notes it sang of a tree beside a waterfall that would be just right for his canoe. As soon as the light dawned, the boy set out to find the waterfall. And sure enough, beside it stood the perfect tree.

The whole while the tree was being hollowed and the paddle carved, the boy's mother cried. She did not want her son to go, but despite her tears and pleas, the day for his journey came. On that day the chief told his son that he was proud of his bravery and that he honored him for following his heart. And even though his mother still sobbed, she kissed him goodbye and wished him good fortune.

Out on the high sea the canoe, which had seemed so large and sturdy in the bay, bobbed over the great ocean as if it were a twig. At times the waves were so high the boy could see only the sky in front of him and then it would seem as if he might dive to the bottom of the sea as it plunged down the great swells. But the canoe, built by his father with such care and knowledge, stayed afloat. Each night he navigated, not by the stars as he'd been taught, but by the voice of love that called him. On the tenth night just as dawn was breaking, his canoe slid ashore on the small, round island. A short time later he presented himself to the king and queen.

"We are honored by your presence," said the king. "The sea god must love you to have allowed you to survive your journey." The king commanded that the boy be an honored guest at the wedding feast being prepared for his twin children.

"I am honored," said the boy, "but first I must go to the great mountain and thank the gods that called me here for guiding me safely."

The chief's son walked back to the sea. He listened for the voice and when he heard it, his heart full, he followed the mountain river through the brush.

At the base of the waterfall he saw the girl twin. Without thinking, he sang in harmony with her. Their heartfelt song floated on the river, out into the ocean and over the sea to the chief and his wife. They smiled knowing their son was safe and happy and that the gods had sent his song to reassure them.

When their song ended, the chief's son said, "I am. . ."

"I know who you are," the girl twin interrupted. "I have sung to you for months."

"Yes, of course," he said smiling. "That is why only I heard your song. Come, let us go back to the village and wed with the royal couple."

The girl told him it was she who was to be wed and that her brother, too, had fallen in love with another. "That is why my songs are so sad," she said. "We cannot defy the wish of the gods or they will put a curse on our island."

"I have come too far to give up now," the chief's son said. "There must be a way."

"I wish it were so," the girl said sadly. "Although I love you deeply, I cannot hurt my parents and the others here."

"Let us find your brother and his love. Together we will appeal to the gods to honor our love."

Off the two went toward the mountain. At its base the girl twin sang a song that she and her brother used to find each other. Soon she heard his answering call.

"He is up there," she said, pointing to the crater rim of the central mountain of the island. "It worries me that he defies the Goddess of Fire by sitting so close to her home."

After a hard climb, they found her twin and the girl from the other side of the mountain. The four embraced and then sat down to figure out a way to stop the wedding.

The girl from the other side of the mountain said, "We have a right to our love. We'll go to the island of the chief's son and live happily ever after."

"But defying the wish of the gods," the girl twin said, "will bring misery and grief to our island."

"There must be a way," the chief's son said.

"We cannot think of one," said the twin boy. His sister nodded.

The girl from the other side of the mountain stood up and, looking down into the crater below, then shouted, "Goddess of Fire, you have known love. Help us to wed the one we love."

"She was disappointed in love. She will not help us," the chief's son said. "But her sister might or one of the other gods might. We will chant the sacred songs and ask for their help."

As their chant rang across the valleys below them, a great rumble shot out of the bowels of the crater.

"We must leave quickly," the chief's son said.

"There is no place to run to," the boy twin answered. "Her liquid fire can scorch every place on the island. We cannot bring harm to the good people of our island."

"We will sing to her of our great love," whispered the girl twin." She is a woman. She will hear us. I know she will."

The four gathered sacred stones and arranged them in a circle, then sat within the circle and held hands. Each in turn sang, and then all four sang together a great chant that touched even the heart of the stones.

"Fire Goddess," the girl twin said, "for love's sake allow us to be together always."

Suddenly, with a loud crack the Fire Goddess appeared before them. Flames flickered from the ends of her hair. Her red gown glowed at its edges with orange embers. The four huddled together inside their circle of stones.

"You are fools to think you can gain love so easily," she roared and the flames in her hair flared. "But the young are always foolish. I suppose you would like to be immortal, too, and live forever."

The boy twin answered, "We would very much like to be together, all four of us, forever." He put his arm around his love and the chief's son did the same with his.

"And what price are you prepared to pay if I grant you this boon?" the Fire Goddess asked. "Such great favors demand great sacrifices."

"Anything, except we cannot hurt the people of our island," the girl twin said.

"We would like our love for each other to bring happiness to this island," the girl from the other side of the mountain added.

The Fire Goddess stared at the brave lovers within their circle of stones. As she thought flames flared from her person. "I can grant your wish to remain together and in granting it serve also the people of this island, but there will be a sacrifice. Are you willing?"

"As long as those two conditions are met, I gladly will fulfill any others," the boy twin said.

"We will, too," chorused the girl twin, the chief's son and the girl from the other side of the mountain.

"So be it," said the Fire Goddess. And in an instant she turned the two couples into stone. "You will always be together each lover entwined with his beloved and seated side by side."

"Your job," the Goddess continued, "will be to trap the clouds as they fly over my mountain so that the people in the valleys below will have enough rain for their trees to bear fruit and their fields to turn green. Only when the fields are as green as emeralds and the fruits of the trees are as brilliant as the finest gold will you be able to regain your human form. But I warn you that as soon as the clouds are empty and leave the peaks of the mountain, you will again be turned to stone. At that moment if you are not in place to catch new clouds, you will be separated from each other and the people in the valley below will suffer. But as long as you do all I have commanded, you will remain immortal, and all who live on this island will be blessed."

And so it was that the lovers became twin peaks on the rim of the great mountain of the Fire Goddess. Even years later, after the Goddess had left the small, round island and taken her fire south to the big island, the four lovers continued to catch the clouds that came in from the sea each day.

And while those clouds clung to the rim of the sacred mountain, pouring rain down its sides to the valleys below, the four were released from their stone bonds to chant and dance and live happily together. And when the clouds were empty and ready to return to the sea to be filled, the four took their places again as stone cloud catchers, content that they would always be together and that they had brought great beauty and happiness to the lush valleys below. And so it continues even to this day.

"... soon she was fast asleep. As she slept the little people of the island, who worked only at night, crept out of the bushes bordering the beach. They had been sent by the Moon Goddess who had told them of the poor girl's plight."

V

The Hibiscus

LONG AGO ON A SMALL, ROUND ISLAND in the middle of the sea a beautiful young girl with long black hair lived with her Auntie and Uncle, who had cared for her ever since her parents died. But now the couple were growing older and felt it was time for her to earn her own way. So one day they packed their canoe and visited the villages along the coast of the island asking if anyone could use her help.

The Queen, who was preparing for a great festival, heard about the girl and sent for her. Now the King and Queen were known to be greedy and hard on their workers. So the Auntie and Uncle did not want their sweet niece to work for such mean people. But what could they do? They were growing old, and the Queen would be very angry if they did not answer her summons.

On a beautiful day when the trade winds blew clouds of dragons across the sky and the palm fronds along the beach danced a graceful hula, they packed their niece's belongings into the canoe. Before she kissed her goodbye, the Auntie gave her niece a beautiful hibiscus flower lei, she'd spent the morning making. As she slipped the lei around her niece's neck, she said, "May these flowers bring you sweet aloha and remind you of our love."

When they reached the King's lands, the Queen stood on the beach, her foot tapping madly. "Where have you been, you lazy girl? We have much work to do." Her uncle barely had time to kiss the child goodbye.

"Come along. Come along," said the Queen as the unhappy girl watched her Uncle's canoe pull away from shore. The niece wiped away a tear and followed the Queen.

"Now, let's see. What can you do?" the Queen said, and then turning, gasped, "Oh my, what a beautiful lei. Leis as pretty as that one would be just perfect for my festival. I will need a thousand.

"But. . .but," the niece said.

"No, buts!" the Queen commanded and clapped her hands three times. From fields and canoes and tops of coconut trees people came running. Everyone was afraid of the Queen's anger.

"Hurry! Hurry!" she ordered. "You must gather all the hibiscus blossoms you can find and bring them to me immediately. And you, get me many sharpened lei needles! You, bring yards and yards of thread!"

"Child," she said to the niece, "you sit down right here. The sea breezes will keep the flowers fresh while you make the leis. If you do a good job and finish them in time for the festival, I will give you a piece of land on which your Auntie, Uncle and you can earn a living. But if you are lazy and do not succeed, you all will die!"

The niece hardly had time to be sad, because soon people came with basket upon basket of flowers, until on the beach there arose a flower mountain of hibiscus blossoms.

"Please," she asked each one as they added their flowers, "please, could you help me I don't know how to make a lei."

"Oh, child, we dare not help," one kind, old lady said. "The Queen has given us all jobs to do. But I will tell you this: thread your needle with string, put it through the heart of the flower and pull it close to the one in front."

The niece pushed back her long hair and picked up a lei needle, and slowly, very slowly started to sew the flowers together with the thick string.

"Ouch. Ouch. Ouch," she'd say, as the needle pricked her finger. By evening she had sewn only three leis, and in the heart of each flower lay a tiny pool of blood from the needle pricks.

As the sun began to sink behind the mountain, she started to cry. How would she ever finish? Through her tears she saw a bright, full moon peek over the edge of the sea. As it rose higher and higher the light from it spread across the water, creating a brilliant moon path right to her feet. Her tearful gaze followed the moon path back to its source and she saw in its white face the beautiful Moon Goddess.

"Oh, Moon Goddess," she cried. "Please help me. My Auntie and Uncle are loving, kind people. I do not want to be the cause of their death. But even if my fingers were not so sore, I could never make a thousand leis in two days."

But the Moon Goddess did not answer. With a sigh, the girl bent her head down and sewed as quickly as she could, her tears mixing with the blood from her fingers. Her head dropped lower and lower until she was fast asleep.

As she slept, Menehunes, the little people of the island, who only worked at night, crept out of the bushes surrounding the beach. They had been sent by the Moon Goddess, who had shone her light on the ditch they were digging and told them of the poor girl's plight. One old fellow, no bigger than a five year old, passed out lei needles, an even tinier, gray-haired woman handed out pieces of string, and the others each grabbed a pile of flowers until the flower mountain had melted into a hundred sand piles of hibiscus blossoms.

Quickly, they got to work. The only noise they made was an occasional "Ouch!" as a needle pricked a tiny finger. In the last moments before the moon stole over the mountain, they pulled down palm branches and hung the leis upon them. Then the weary Menehunes dipped their sore fingers in the sea and trudged off to bed.

In the morning the sun blazed its light over the ocean and woke the weary girl.

"Oh dear, I fell asleep," she cried, jumping up and splashing sea water on her face. Wearily, she turned back to her impossible task. But where the mountain of flowers had been, she now saw branch after branch of palm fronds encircled with hibiscus leis that danced in the breeze. "Oh, what miracle is this?" she asked, touching lei after lei.

"Did I do this in my sleep?" she wondered, because in the center of each blossom lay a tiny pool of blood. "Oh, that could never be. I do not have enough blood to fill all of these flowers.

"Oh Moon Goddess, thank you, *thank you* for your help."

When the Queen came to the beach, she said nothing to the girl, but went to examine the leis.

"These blossoms have blood in them," she screamed. "I cannot have bloody leis at my festival. You must remove this blood at once!"

So the poor girl spent the day washing the hibiscus blossoms in the sea. But as each blossom was washed clean of the blood in its center, it died. When the Queen came again, and saw the dead blossoms she turned red with anger. She clapped her hands three times, and again the people came from their work, and again she sent them for hibiscus blossoms. By the time the sun had crept behind the clouds gathered at the peak of the mountain, the flowers towered to the treetops.

"You'd better do it right this time, you stupid girl," the Queen warned.

Later, when the moon rose from the depth of the sea, the girl called to the Moon Goddess. "Please, you helped me before, could you help me again." Then she dropped her head to the sand and soon was asleep. Again the Menehunes came from their labors, and put their sore fingers to work, and the next morning there were hundreds more leis decorating the palm fronds. The girl leapt up and ran to look at the leis. But again, sadly, in the center of each was a tiny pool of blood.

"You horrible child," the Queen screamed when she saw them. "If you have no leis for my festival tomorrow, you, your Auntie and Uncle will die!" She clapped her hands and for the third time sent the people to gather blossoms. But there were no blossoms left on that side of the mountain, and it would be well past moonrise by the time the people reached the other side.

When the Moon Goddess returned that night and heard from the girl that the Queen was still dissatisfied, she turned to the sea and in a thunderous voice ordered a great storm to arise. Before a single blossom could be picked, the skies darkened and the rains came. But this was no ordinary storm. The fury of the Moon Goddess had turned the rain red, and all the night and the next day it poured. Red rain flooded the land, filling the hibiscus blossoms and coloring the earth.

Of course, the Queen's festival was completely ruined. The people of the village, wanting to regain favor with the Moon Goddess and stop the storm, forced the King and Queen from their throne. In their place the people chose the girl's good Auntie and Uncle.

When the Moon Goddess heard that the wicked Queen and King were gone, she stopped the blood rain, but ordered that from that day forth the island earth would be stained red, and the center of each hibiscus blossom would hold a spot of blood to remind the people always to keep the spirit of aloha in their hearts.

"The boy sang to the gentle heave of the giant's breathing until he had sung every song he knew. Still humming he stretched his arm to lift the giant's eyelid just a bit to see if he was really sleeping."

VI

Sleeping Giant

ONG AGO WHEN GIANTS STILL WALKED THE EARTH, one of the large fellows came to visit a small, round island in the sea. The villagers of the island fed the giant whenever he yelled for food, because in this land it was wrong to allow any to go hungry. But this giant ate so much and complained so loudly that soon the villagers were spending all their time feeding him and had no time to gather food for themselves.

"What can we do?" the village elders asked each other.

"He seems perfectly content to remain here forever," said one.

"Let's ask our wise man if he knows of some way to get rid of this fellow," another suggested.

The wise man listened gravely as they told of their plight.

After a long silence he spoke, "Although this giant has been greedy and is causing our people much misery, we cannot break the spirit of our land and refuse him food. To do so would bring down the wrath of the gods, who would cause the fish to leave the sea, and the fruit to wither on the trees. You must find another way to persuade this fellow to share our bounty or go."

"But what way?" they asked.

"There is a way," he answered quietly, "but answers are only true when you discover them for yourself."

That night after the giant had finally stopped eating and gone to sleep, the elders called all the villagers to the beach. Everyone gathered around a newly-carved canoe. The elders repeated the wise man's reply.

"Any man, woman, or child who can offer a solution to this puzzle will be rewarded with this beautiful canoe," the oldest elder declared.

Soon the beach buzzed as the villagers exchanged ideas.

One man rubbed his hand along the polished hull of the canoe and said to his wife and three sons, "We must find the answer."

To his first son, he said, "You are strong. Use your strength."

To his second son, he said, "You are clever. Use your brain."
"Yes, father," they answered. "But what about him? What will he use?" Both boys laughed as they pointed their fingers at their

youngest brother, who was staring at the stars and singing to himself.

"Leave him alone," the father said. "He's still small and not much use."

All the next day and the day after the villagers tried their tricks to stop the giant from eating. By the third day they were exhausted, and still the giant demanded, "Food. Food. I'm starving!"

The two brothers decided to work together. They were sure with the oldest one's strength and the middle one's brains, they would find the answer. The younger one asked if he might help, but they only laughed and told him he was too simple-minded and weak to be of any help.

"What would you do?" laughed the clever one. "Sing to him?"

The young one nodded sadly. What could he do when everyone else so much bigger and smarter had failed?

On the third day the two brothers came up with a plan.

"You will bring all the big rocks you can find to the beach," the clever brother said to the strong one, "and I will fix him a meal he'll never forget."

When the strong brother arrived at the beach, the clever one was mixing a giant pot of soup brewed with fresh fish, fruit and taro.

"Now break those stones up into smaller chunks," the clever one commanded, "and I will mix them in with the soup. The giant will eat our stew and feel very full. Very full indeed. Then we will challenge him to a swim in the ocean. He will be so heavy from his supper, he surely will drown in the current."

"That new canoe is as good as ours," the strong one said. "Won't father be proud of us?"

The younger brother, singing softly, came up to the two as they worked. "Can I help? Please?" he asked.

"Go away!" they shouted together.

Humming a sad tune, he went down the beach a little way and lay down on the sand to sing to the stars. He wondered if he would ever be big enough, strong enough, and clever enough to win a canoe for his father.

Meanwhile, his brothers found the giant and told him to come to the beach. "We've prepared a delicious stew full of the good things of the earth and sea," the clever one said.

Although the giant had just eaten, he belched a few times, punched his fat belly hard to make some room and followed them to the beach.

They stirred the huge pot of food and handed him the ladle. The giant sat down, his legs straddling either side of the pot, and slurped huge spoonfuls down his massive throat. His belly got bigger and bigger. It rumbled and roared. The two brothers put their hands over their mouths to stifle their giggles. When the pot was almost empty, the giant picked it up in his hands, raised it to his mouth and greedily poured the rest down his throat. A belch rose up from his belly and out his mouth with such ferocity that the palms bent in its blast until their tops touched the sand. The noise brought all the villagers to the beach just in time to watch the brothers carry out their plan.

"I hear you are a pretty good swimmer," the clever brother said to the giant, who was too full to do anything but nod. "My brother is the strongest swimmer on the island. He says he can beat you."

"Hah!" the giant huffed, and the effort started another huge belch rolling up from his stomach and out his mouth with a roar. The villagers clapped their hands over their ears and dug their feet in the sand. The palm fronds brushed their backs, and the smell made them wish for yet another hand to hold their noses.

"I guess you're too full to race him, huh?" the clever brother asked.

The giant looked as if he were about to be sick, which caused the villagers to scurry to higher ground. With a moan the giant stood, but quickly he dropped back down, doubled over, holding his stomach. He was very sick.

"How about our race?" the strong brother shouted.

The giant's only answer was another belch. The force of this one pushed the strong brother and many of the curious villagers into the sea.

"That was a really dumb idea," the strong brother said to the clever one, as they both tread water. "Maybe you're not so clever, after all."

"And maybe you're not so strong, either," the clever brother retorted, "or you'd have reached shore by now."

Meanwhile, the giant sat in the field at the foot of the big mountain in the center of the island, holding his belly and moaning.

The youngest brother, who had scampered off the beach after the first belch, heard the giant moan and went to him. He tapped the giant on the shin and then ducked because the giant, thinking him a fly, swatted at him.

"Hey," the boy yelled. "What's the matter? Are you sick?"

The giant could only nod, because another huge belch was coming. The boy ducked behind the giant's leg and held onto the thick black hairs growing on it.

When the belch subsided, the giant muttered, "Must've been something I ate."

"My brothers aren't very good cooks," the boy said. "When I have a sick stomach my mother puts me to bed and sings me songs until I fall asleep. Maybe if I sang you a song you could fall asleep and your stomach would be all better in the morning."

The giant heaved a loud sigh and stretched out in the field at the foot of the mountain. "Sing away, boy," he ordered.

The boy climbed up onto the giant's hand, and then walked through the jungle of hair on the giant's arms to the thicker jungle of hair on his chest.

Using the giant's beard as ropes he climbed up to the giant's chin. From there he walked through his beard to a clear perch on the giant's cheek bone. And then he sang.

In the middle of his second song the giant yawned and the singing brother almost slid off. But he grabbed an eyelash just in time. Soon the giant's belly stopped rumbling. The boy sang to the gentle heave of the giant's breathing until he had sung every song he knew. Still humming, he stretched his arm to lift the giant's eyelid just a tiny bit to see if he was really sleeping. Sure enough, the giant was fast asleep.

The boy climbed down and ran to tell his family. Of course, his brothers didn't believe his songs put the giant to sleep. They were sure it was their stone soup.

The next day the villagers were relieved that the giant stayed asleep and demanded no more food. But when the boy asked for the prize canoe, they laughed.

"Don't be silly," one of the elders said. "When he wakes up, he'll be hungrier than ever."

But after a week, he was still fast asleep. Another, and another week passed. The earth turned warm and then the rains came, but still the giant slept. Soon grass and flowers grew on him. The next year trees sprouted from his body. By the time the boy was almost grown, people would climb the giant for a Sunday afternoon hike.

"Now may I have my canoe?" the boy asked.

The elders looked thoughtfully at each other.

"The giant has not awakened," said one.

"But he only sang him to sleep," said another.

"Still, the giant does not trouble us. Instead he gives us pleasure climbing him," said another.

So on the next sunny day the elders gathered all the villagers in the grassy field of the giant's forehead to honor the boy who had soothed the giant to sleep with a song. Afterward they all went to the beach to help the boy push his new canoe into the water.

From that day until he died an old man, the boy fished and sang, bringing food and pleasure to his family and village. And the villagers spent many pleasurable hours climbing the sleeping giant, now covered with trees, grass and flowers, to enjoy the view of the sea from his forehead.

And from that time forward to this day, the people of that small, round island in the middle of the sea have known the value of a song and will stop to listen whenever and wherever one is sung.

" A great piercing cry rose from the whale . . . The huge whale soared above the water with Lani riding on its flipper."

VII

In The Belly Of The Whale

LONG AGO AND FAR AWAY on a small, round island in the middle of the sea, there lived a couple with six big sons and one small daughter. The father had never been very successful at providing for his large brood because he was a dreamer who spent his time by the edge of the sea singing songs and telling stories to his small daughter, Lani. Often he would make up stories about the crazy whale who lived in the bay and who, unlike other whales, did not migrate, but lived year 'round out beyond the reef.

"Stop filling that child's head with foolishness," his wife would scold. "You should be fishing. We have many mouths to feed. Get busy!"

Often, to silence her nagging, he would push his canoe into the water and paddle out beyond the breakers, where not even her loudest shriek could carry. Then he would lie back in his canoe and while away the hours creating a song. On the beach his little Lani would wait patiently for his return.

But one day, when his wife's nagging had chased him out to sea, his canoe drifted out over the reef. He never noticed how far he'd moved until the crazy whale loomed over him. When it flopped back down with a mighty crash, it sent him flying out of his canoe into the sea.

In the dim light of the underwater world he saw the jaws of the whale open as if waiting for him. He tried to swim against the strong current pulling him into that huge whale cavern. But his years of idleness had made him weak. With a great rush of water, seaweed and tiny fish, he was swept through the jaws and down into the belly of the whale.

There he floundered about in the darkness, his arms tangled in seaweed. Suddenly a great force, a muscle in the beast's belly heaved in a spasm and threw him into a small, dry chamber. He crawled around feeling the warm, living floor beneath his hands and knees. In a rounded corner, his hands touched what felt like a pile of wood. Choosing two pieces that seemed dry, he rubbed them together. After a long time rubbing, he raised a spark which soon blazed into fire.

The fire illuminated a small chamber open at the far end. He looked around and saw some matting from which he could fashion a bed. Beyond the matting lay coconuts, fish and fruits, as if someone had planned a supper for him. He cooked the fish over his fire, then sat down on his matting and ate it with the fruit, washing it all down with coconut milk. He belched a few times and felt so content he sang his favorite songs. By the time he was ready to sleep he felt quite at home.

But back on shore, the man's tiny daughter had seen his canoe flip over and alerted her mother and brothers. They gathered the other people of the village and searched for him until the shadow of their island mountain turned the sea black.

During the night his empty canoe washed up on the beach. Days passed without his return. All, except Lani, assumed he had drowned. Each day Lani sat by the edge of the sea and watched the place where her father had disappeared.

Her mother complained when Lani would forget to fetch driftwood for their fire, "You are as lazy as he was. Pretty songs and silly stories never fed an empty belly." But still the child watched the sea, waiting for her father.

Meanwhile, in the belly of the whale, her father quite liked his new home. The whale provided him with food and wood. No one nagged him or interrupted his songs or stories. And he told his stories and sang his songs aloud because it seemed to him the whale listened. After a while, the whale even sang along with him in its high-pitched voice. Within a few weeks, the two understood each other completely. The father's happiness would have been total, except for one thing. He missed his little Lani.

The whale asked in his singing voice, "Why are your songs sad? I have given you a nice dry home and plenty to eat."

The father answered, "I am grateful for your gifts and I would be happy here if I did not miss my daughter."

"That beautiful child on the beach?" the whale asked.

"Yes. And she is as sweet as she is beautiful. If only I could see her, I would be happy and content."

"I will find a way," the whale sang. Its tail swished back and forth as it thought and thought. The father, rocked in his chamber by the back and forth movement of the tail, grew quite seasick. He was about to beg the whale to stop, when suddenly it did stop.

The whale bellowed, "I have it! Swim up into my mouth and wedge yourself between my gum and lip." The father dove out of his chamber and did as he was told. "Now hold fast," the whale warned. "We are going up." With that it rose from the depths of the ocean floor until its body was half out of the water.

The father, grasping tightly to the whale's lower lip, trembled as they rose. Once in the air the whale twisted its body and the father, squinting his eyes, saw his little Lani sitting on the beach staring straight toward them.

"Now are you happy?" sang the whale as they plunged back down into the depths.

"I would be it she did not look so sad," the father said. "She must believe I have drowned. I must show her I am fine."

"All right," sang the whale. "Hold tight. We're going up again." This time it breached even higher. Its whole length cleared the surface of the water until it seemed as if it were standing on its tail. The father let go of the whale's lip and waved his arms and shouted.

Lani saw and heard him. She jumped up and with her arms outstretched ran straight into the sea. Without a backward look she splashed toward the place where they had plunged back into the water.

"Now are you happy?" asked the whale as they glided back to the surface of the sea.

"I would be," the father said, "but look how far from shore Lani is. I never taught her to swim. She surely will drown."

With that, the whale opened his mighty jaws and swam toward the child. Lani, spotting her father clinging to the whale's lip, lifted her arms and shouted with joy, which caused her to swallow water and sink. Her father wriggled free from his perch and dropped to catch her. The whale with a deep gulp of water swooped them both into his mouth. They flowed through his mouth and into his belly, where the whale twitched his muscle and pushed them into the dry chamber.

As soon as Lani caught her breath she danced around the chamber shouting, "Father! Father! I am so happy. I knew you were alive. I knew it. I love you. I love you."

"Now?" cried the whale.

The father caught Lani in his arms and shouted, "Yes! Now I am completely happy. Thank you, my great friend."

For the next few years the father and daughter lived quite contentedly in the belly of the whale. For school Lani's father taught her songs, even helped her compose a few of her own, and told her tales of the island gods. For fun, the whale taught her to swim and surf the far reef. After her lessons, the whale would take Lani for rides. She would grasp its flipper and off they would go, streaking through the water. Eventually, she could hold fast even when the whale breached. How she loved flying through the air with him. Once in a while someone surfing or fishing near the reef would spot them, but Lani didn't care. She was happy.

Years passed. Lani grew from a little girl into a young woman. Her father noticed that she seemed less contented, even restless. "Lani, what's wrong?" he asked.

"Father, I have loved being here with you and the whale, but how will I find a husband in the belly of a whale? I think it's time for me to go back to land and marry."

Her father sadly realized that his little girl had become a woman and it was time for her to leave home and find a husband. He spoke with the whale about it. The whale, too, felt sad--very sad--at the thought of her leaving. But the two knew in their hearts that Lani was right.

Early one morning the whale swam in close to the beach and sent Lani shoreward on a wave. When her family and villagers asked her where she had been all these years, she said only, "I went to live with my father, and now I've come back."

"Crazy as her fool father," they whispered to each other.

"All that singing and storytelling weakened her brain," her practical mother explained.

Many of the young men also suspected Lani was the girl they'd seen clinging to the crazy whale in the bay. So despite Lani's beauty and lovely songs, none wanted to marry her. And although Lani was lonely, she found no young man that pleased her, either. Often she would walk by the sea and watch for her whale friend. The whale, too, was lonely for Lani. He often swam close to shore to see her. Whenever he saw her he would send a great spout of water high into the air as a greeting and then lift a mighty flipper so his eye would stay above sea level.

One day the whale swam close by, his eye watching Lani. She dove into the sea and swam out to him. The whale opened its great jaws and with a happy rush of sea she floated into his mouth and down to her father's dry chamber. After much rejoicing, she told the whale and her father about how she had been treated.

"I will just stay here with the two of you," she said, "and except for not having a husband and children, I will be very happy."

"Lani, I would love to have you here," her father said. "But it is time for you to marry and have children. I am getting old. I want to see you settled before I die."

"If you wish, I could take you to another island," the whale sang. "Once there you could say you were swept overboard and swam ashore."

Lani, with a sad heart, agreed to their plan. A few days later the whale swam southward to a neighboring island, leaving Lani near a beach at dawn. Once ashore, Lani told the story the others had suggested. Within a few days many of the handsome young men of the island came to woo her. She attended their feasts and surfed the high waves with them, but always her eyes scanned the sea looking for the whale. Occasionally, she would see a whale swimming by or breaching, but none spouted her whale's special greeting or had flukes spotted the same as her whale.

And that was because her father and the whale had returned to their home in the bay. The whale had explained to her father that one of the old goddesses of the sea had put a special curse on him. To break it he needed to stay in that bay. Otherwise he would have wished to stay near Lani.

When the father asked the whale to tell him the whole story, the whale sadly refused. "If I tell," the whale explained, "I will be doomed to this spot forever."

The father honored his friend's need to keep his secret. But each day the whale seemed sadder and sadder. His keening songs filled the depths of the sea. He rarely breached, and when he went to the surface he sent only a tiny spume of water over his blow hole.

Now it was the father's turn to be the comforter. "My friend, what is troubling you? You have given me many happy years here in your belly. Let me help you now."

"I wish you could," sang the whale, "but I fear my sadness cannot be cured."

"But you were so happy when Lani was here with us."

A great keening cry rose from the whale and echoed through the bay.

"Oh, I see," said the father.

Over the next few weeks the father complained often of feeling sick. He told the whale that he feared he might be dying and asked if the whale might consider taking him to see Lani one last time. The whale, although he knew it was dangerous to flout the command of the sea goddess once again, agreed to take him.

They arrived at dawn. The whale swam back and forth looking for Lani. At noon he spotted her, surfboard under her arm, coming down the beach with a group of young people. He watched until he saw her look out to sea, then slapped his flukes and sent a spout of water as high as a palm tree into the air.

Lani stopped in her tracks. She ran into the water with her board and quickly paddled out. Her friends, startled by her furious paddling, watched from shore as she swam straight to the whale. Once there she let go of her board and grabbed the whale's flipper. Her friends, bent on rescuing her, launched into the waves on their boards.

"I'm so happy to see you. I've missed you," Lani cried over and over, trying to hug the smooth gray skin of the whale's side.

"I have missed you, too," the whale sang softly.

"Why did you leave?" she asked. "I looked for you every day."

"I cannot stay here," the whale said. "I am under a spell of enchantment."

"What? Why didn't you tell me this before?" she asked.

"Because it is sad for a whale to stay alone close to land. You are so tenderhearted, I didn't want you to be sad for me. Besides, when you were with me, I forgot my sadness and loneliness."

"Poor whale," she said, patting it. "You have been so kind to my father and me."

"It gave me joy," he sang. "Tell me, from among your friends have you found a husband?"

"No. I cannot find a man I love, although many here profess to love me."

"There is no one you love?" the whale's voice sounded happy.

"Yes, there is someone I love, but not a man," she said softly. She felt the whale tremble. "I love one who is kind and good, but cannot give me children." She laid her head against its slick wet skin and pressed her lips to a spot above its flipper. "I love only you and my father."

A great piercing cry rose from the whale. The sound swept over the water to the approaching surfers. They turned their boards swiftly and paddled in terror back to the shore. Two of them who looked back saw the huge whale soar high above the water with Lani riding on its flipper.

When at last its joy could be contained, the whale swooped Lani inside to see her father. As Lani confided in her father about her love for their friend, the whale swam them back to his island bay.

Night had fallen when they reached it, and a full moon lit it with silvery sparkles. After Lani's father fell asleep, she and the whale drifted upon the sea quite close to shore. She told him that her father was pleased she loved someone as good and kind as the whale. It was almost dawn when the whale gathered his courage and sang, "I love you, Lani. I wish you to be my wife."

"I will be your wife," Lani said. "We may not have children, but we will have songs and love."

With that the world burst into light. The silver of the night became the gold of the day. A huge wave rose far into the sky. Lani closed her eyes and floated up on it. As she drifted down the other side she reached out to the whale. But she touched a man. She opened her eyes and saw floating beside her a handsome, bronzed youth. She dove underwater to look for her whale, but saw nothing in the clear, calm water. Sputtering to the surface, she found not only the handsome youth, but also her father looking robust and laughing loudly.

"The whale. Where did he go?" she cried.

"I am the whale, or was," sang the young man. She recognized the whale's voice. "I was doomed to live in this bay as a whale until a woman of this island would marry me. You see, many long years ago, my father stole the daughter of the sea goddess. The sea goddess swore that their first born child would be hers. My father was so happy that he forgot about the curse. But one day while I was learning to surf, the goddess caught me, turned me into a whale and told me I could never walk on earth again until I found a maiden of the island who would marry me as a whale. I have stayed close to this island, hoping against hope to find just such a woman. You, my beautiful Lani, have given me back my earth life."

Swiftly the three swam to shore, and that very night gathered the islanders to the beach for the wedding. Her father sang a song during the wedding feast about the curse of the whale that was lifted by love.

That night as Lani and her handsome husband snuggled together on the land, she whispered, "I will miss our life in the sea, but I will be happy on land with you."

Her husband looked deeply into her eyes and said, "I have another secret to tell. One, which by the goddess' command I could not tell you before the wedding. I am still part of sea, because my grandmother was a goddess of the sea. Every year for six months I must live my life in the sea as a whale."

"When that time comes, I will gladly go with you," Lani said. "And when our children are born they, too, will go."

"That is good," he sang as he hugged her, "because our children will also be whales part of the year."

With that matter settled, the two started their married life. In summer they lived in a small cottage beside the sea, but in winter, they and their children would disappear. No one knew where.

And to this day, just off the coast of this small, round island in the middle of the sea, you can see descendants of Lani and the whale during the winter months. As they swim past the island, they greet their home with high sprays of water and slap their speckled flukes. And in the water if you listen carefully, the keening love song of Lani's whale can still be heard.

"And even today in the skies of the small, round island, you can see the happy couple when the sun of the sea and the mist of the mountains meet together in ribbons the color of the earth and sky."

VIII

The Rainbow

NCE UPON A TIME on a small round island, where the mountains live close to the sea, the people of the mountains and the people of the sea were at war. Because of the war the people of the sea no longer could go to the mountains to gather wood to make boats and paddles. And the mountain people could not go to the sea for the fish they loved to eat. Everyone was unhappy.

A man living between these two warring tribes feared for the safety of his wife and baby daughter. So one day he took his wife by the hand and wrapped his daughter in a tapa cloth and climbed the steep mountain to find a safer home for his family. Just as they were about to reach the top, the tapa cloth split open and the baby girl fell down through the mountain mist toward the sea.

In those days the gods of the sea and sky still walked the earth. The Goddess of the Sun saw the tiny child hurtling to the sea through the fine mountain mist and caught her in her arms. Her parents could see nothing below but mist filled with the colors of the ocean, earth and sky.

The girl child grew into a beautiful maiden with hair the color of the sea and mountains. Each day she sat beside a deep mountain pool and sang with the waterfall that kept the pool full and fresh.

One by one the people of the mountain came upon her and listened to her wise songs. Soon they came to her when they were troubled and needed advice. They told her of their sadness in not being able to eat the fresh fish of the sea.

Meanwhile the people of the sea complained that without paddles made from the mountain trees they could not use their boats and had to be satisfied with catching the little fish that swam close to shore. They asked their chief to hold a feast so they could again be happy. But the chief refused saying, there would be no feast until his son took a wife. The people went to the son urging him to marry, but he said he had seen all the women of the tribe and could find none that he loved.

A small child told the chief's son that once he had heard beautiful singing from the mountains and had climbed part way up, even though it was forbidden, to find the singer. He then described the beautiful maiden with all the colors of the sea and mountain in her hair.

"I must see this woman for myself," the chief's son declared and so he set off to where the boy said he could be found. Soon he heard her voice and followed it until he saw her sitting in the mist beside her waterfall. Her beauty enchanted him. His heart felt as if a thousand spears pierced it.

"Come with me, beautiful one," he called. "Be my wife."

"I will if you can tell my name," she sang.

"But how can I know your name," he asked, "if we have never met?"

"And how can I marry a man who does not know my name."

The chief's son left downcast and disheartened. He pined and pined, refusing to eat or talk. The Chief and his wife grew worried. They sent for the Goddess of The Sun.

"Tell us," they begged, "what can we do to help him? He will die if he does not eat."

"What is troubling you, my boy?" the Goddess of the Sun asked so sweetly that not even one so unhappy could keep silent.

He told her of the beautiful maiden and her refusal to wed him unless he knew her name.

"I know her name," the Goddess said, "and if you will eat and grow strong and make your people happy, I will tell it to you."

Every minute of every day the chief's son strengthened his body with food, play, and work. And soon he was more handsome than he had ever been. He called for the Goddess of the Sun.

When she saw him, she smiled. "You are now ready to wed."

"Tell me quickly," he begged, "the name of my beloved."

"She is the meeting of the mist from the mountain with the sun of the sea. That is all I can tell you. You must trust your love to give you the rest."

Suddenly the chief's son laughed loudly. "I know. *I know,*" he shouted and ran off toward the mountains.

When he found her singing beside the waterfall, he called, "Rainbow. Beautiful Rainbow, will you marry me and make our people happy again?"

"You have guessed my name," she sang. "Yes, I will marry you."

The next day all the people of the mountain brought wood to the people of the sea, and the people of the sea brought fish to the people of the mountain. And the following day they all met in peace beside the clear, deep pool that lay at the foot of the singing waterfall to share in the wedding and feast of the chief's son and Rainbow. And even today in the skies of the small, round island one can see the happy couple when the sun of the sea and the mist of the mountains meet together in ribbons the color of the earth and the sky.

"(Kimo) stared straight at the bone cave, stood tall to gather his strength into the spear and drew his arm back. But before he let his spear fly, he prayed, 'Spirit of this land, help me right the wrong I have commited.'"

IX

The Fire Thrower

NCE UPON A TIME on a small, round island in the middle of the sea, there lived a kind old couple who, despite their desire for children, were never blessed with them. Then one day a great tidal wave struck the island. A whole family was carried out to sea and drowned. Only their newborn child was washed back onto the shore. The couple found him, named him Kimo, and raised him as their own.

Because they had waited so long for a child, the couple could deny him nothing. Kimo spent his days playing and getting into mischief. Often as he left their cottage for the beach, his surfboard under his arm, the old couple would say that soon the time would come when Kimo would accept the burdens of manhood.

One day Kimo came home with a bone dangling from a rolled ti leaf he had tied around his neck. His father examined it, then recoiled in horror.

"That's a bone from a human finger," he said. "Kimo, where did you get it?"

"Oh, some of the big boys dared me to climb down the cliff side to the bone cave. They said if I brought back a bone they would take me pig-hunting."

"Oh, Kimo," his father's voice trembled. "That is the resting place of a mighty sorcerer, one of our ancient holy men.

"Father, I do not believe in the old ways," Kimo said.

"But, Kimo, a burial place is sacred. When you disturb it, you disturb the spirit of the soul buried there. Have you no sense of respect?"

"Father, those ideas are from the old days," Kimo said. "Dead people are just dead. Besides, I only took one little bone. What harm can it do? He'll never miss it." Kimo smiled his most charming smile.

"Maybe he is right," his mother said. "These are new times with new ways."

But his father would hear none of it. "You have disturbed a strong spirit. It will let you know its presence is wandering the land."

"That's silly, father. This bone will be my lucky charm. Now the other boys respect me. Just watch. I bet I will trap the largest boar on our pig hunt."

But when it came time for the hunt, the other families would not allow their sons to go with Kimo because he still wore the bone. It made him so angry, he decided to go alone. His mother begged him not to, but his father knew it was time Kimo earned the name of hunter.

"You must only kill the adult male, the boar; not the sow or the young pigs," the father said. "The boar offers us sport as well as meat. To kill the young or the sow is forbidden."

"Yes, yes, father," the boy answered impatiently.

With his spear over his shoulder, Kimo headed up the trail into the mountains. He climbed higher and higher until he reached a place where the trees grew tall and spread their branches together overhead, giving him only a glimpse of the sky. After a while he grew weary. Hunger gnawed at his stomach. Looking around for a fruit tree, he spotted one heavy with plums and reached for the fruit. A sudden gust blew the branch out of reach. He tried again and again. Each time, just as he was about to pluck one, a gust blew and the plum eluded him. Puzzled, he gave up and walked on.

A little further up the trail, he came to a small waterfall. He cupped his hands under it, and a gust of wind drove the water out of reach.

"What is happening here?" he wondered, and his hand rose to the bone hanging from his neck. Was his father right? Could this be the work of an angry sorcerer? He yanked at the leaf holding the bone, but it refused to break. He tried to slip it over his head, but the circle was too small. Hungry and thirsty, and by now a little scared, he picked up his spear and walked on. The woods grew darker and thicker.

Just when he was about to give up and head back down the trail to home, he heard the snort of a wild pig. He hid in a thicket and watched and listened. Soon he saw coming toward him an old sow and three young pigs. He remembered what his father had said about killing only the male pigs, but without food or water, he would have to go back, and he did not wish to go back without a pig.

He raised his spear, took aim at the sow, and threw it. The spear, which had seemed headed for the sow's heart, stopped midway and dropped with a thud on the ground. The sow snorted angrily. Kimo grabbed a stone and heaved it in her direction, but it, too, flew halfway and then dropped onto the spear with a clang. Kimo's hand reached for the bone. The leaf would not yield.

The sow pawed the ground and then charged Kimo. In terror he tore through the forest, not caring about keeping to the path. When he finally dropped, exhausted, he was lost. Through a tiny clearing in the trees he could see in the patch of sky overhead the red clouds of evening. He grabbed the bone, sure by now, that it was the source of his misfortune, and yanked it hard. The leaf held fast.

"Sorcerer, hear me," he cried. "I promise to return your bone to its cave as soon as I get back." He listened. Nothing. "I'm sorry for my disrespect."

"You violated my tomb," said a deep voice driven by the wind. "You must atone."

"I will. I will," said Kimo. "Anything you wish, I will do."

"You must perform three tasks," the voice in the wind roared, making Kimo shiver. "If you complete all three by morning, you may return home. But if you fail, you will never live as a man."

Kimo nodded.

"First, you must find a home built only by mouth," the voice commanded. "Go now. I will tell you the others after you find it."

"But how can a house be built only with the mouth?" Kimo asked.

"Use your brain and your heart, boy, or you will never live as a man." With a loud rustle of leaves, the wind died.

Kimo thought and thought, but he had no idea what kind of house could be built by mouth. He called for the sorcerer to ask him more questions, but in response he heard only the squawk of a bird. Kimo rose and walked toward the sound. In the ferns he saw a young bird, flapping its still useless wings.

Kimo looked up into the trees overhead for the nest, but their tops were so high, it was out of sight. He shrugged and walked away. The baby bird squawked loudly. Looking up, Kimo saw the mother bird circling overhead.

Although thoughtless, he was a kind boy. He turned and scooped up the baby. Searching the treetops more thoroughly, he spotted a nest out on the end of a limb. With the bird in one hand, he used the other and his feet to climb the tree, not at all sure he would make it.

After a long climb, he came to the branch with the nest. He inched out along the limb, praying it would not crack. Above him the giant bird circled, watching. The limb creaked and dipped under his weight as he crawled closer and closer. When he could reach it with his hand, he stretched out his arm and placed the baby bird in the nest. Just as he did, the giant bird swooped down toward him carrying a piece of dried grass in her mouth.

"That's it!" Kimo shouted. "A *bird* builds its home with its mouth."

"Just so," he heard the voice in the wind. "But that is only one."

Kimo scampered down the tree, feeling much better. "Tell me the next one."

"You must find the creature that is born twice, but dies only once."

"Impossible," Kimo complained, "Every creature is born once and dies once."

"Foolish boy," roared the wind. "You know nothing!"

Kimo set off through the forest listening carefully, hoping he might find the answer to this next riddle as he had the first. By now the forest was darkening. What if he did not have enough time to complete all three?

At the edge of the forest, he came upon a mountain rooster crowing as he called his hens to roost. Hens scurried from all directions followed by their chicks. Just as the last family was about to settle down, a great rat sneaked from the brush and grabbed a chick. Kimo dove for the rat, which dropped the chick, then bit him. Rubbing his sore hand, Kimo placed the chick beside the rooster, who chased it into the roost. As the mother hen moved to make room, Kimo saw an egg beneath her crack.

"That's number two!" he cried. "A chicken is born first as an egg and then as a bird. So it's born twice and dies only once."

"You have done well, boy," the voice in the wind said. "But the next one will not be as easy. You must find the thing that eats as long as it lives, but when it drinks, dies. When you have found it you must attach my bone to it and make it fly back to its resting place."

Even though the request confused him, Kimo trusted that again the answer would appear to him. He walked swiftly along, listening, watching and thinking. Far below he saw smoke rising from a fire. As he hurried toward it, he realized that a fire lives as long as you feed it wood, but dies when it is given water. But this time he did not shout triumphantly, because he had no idea how to make the fire fly.

With the wind blowing stiffly at his back and clearing a path before him through the brush he descended the mountain. Halfway down at the edge of a cliff he reached a fire and found a group of men from the village sitting about it.

"What are you doing here, boy?" one of the men demanded.

"It's Kimo, the one who stole the bone from the sorcerer's cave," another said, drawing back from him. "You must leave before we are all blamed for your foolishness. You have caused your old father much grief."

"I know I have been foolish," Kimo said softly. "I begged the sorcerer's forgiveness and he gave me three tasks to complete."

"Well, get on with it, boy," the first man said.

"I'm not sure what I'm to do. The sorcerer gives me my tasks in riddles, and I must figure them out. I know that he sent me to find your fire, but he also told me to attach this bone to the fire and make it fly to its place in the bone cave."

"This is the night of the fire throw, boy," the second man said.

"Fire throw?" Kimo asked. "How do you throw fire?"

"It is an old custom of the men of our island to come once a year to this high cliff and set four spears aflame and see who can send his the furthest out on the river below. Fire throwing takes a clear mind, a strong will, and great strength. You spend your time surfing and do not even throw a spear well. How could you throw one across the valley to that bone cave?"

Kimo said nothing. Quickly, he gathered all the branches he could find that could be made into spears. He found a stone with an edge and sharpened it with another. As the men laughed and told stories of great fire-throwing feats from bygone days, Kimo worked on his spears. When he had four ready, he asked an old man to teach him how to throw it.

"You must look straight ahead and see your target clearly. Do not follow the spear as it flies," the old man said.

Kimo readied his spear and stared at the bone cave, lit by the moon. From across the valley, the dark outline of the cave entrance formed the shape of a dancing Tiki god, the god the villagers worshiped in the old days. Kimo shuddered. He stared at the fearsome shape and threw the spear with all his might. It curved in an arc and fell to the valley below.

"You must draw your arm straight back, put all your might into the thrust," the old man continued.

Again Kimo prepared a spear and stared ahead at his target. This time he pulled his arm straight back. His spear went further, and did not curve, but still fell to earth before reaching the bone cave.

"You must stand tall as a man to gather your strength into the spear," said the old man.

This time Kimo threw the spear with such force it clattered against the stone above the cave.

"You have only one spear left, boy," the old man said. "You must attach the bone to it and pray that the spirit of this land will guide it."

Kimo walked away from the others, and tugged at the leaf that circled his neck. This time the leaf gave way. He secured the bone by winding the leaf around it and his spear, then dipped it in the fire. Slowly, he walked to the edge of the cliff, stared straight at the bone cave, stood tall to gather his strength into the spear and pulled his arm straight back.

But before he let his spear fly, he prayed, "Spirit of this land, help me right the wrong I have committed." With a mighty thrust, he sent the spear across the valley. It flew straight and true. The men scrambled to their feet to watch. The spear entered the cave, as if piercing the dancing Tiki's heart. The fire throwers gasped at the boy's skill. From below where the other villagers watched there came a cheer. Kimo raised his arms and thanked the spirit for guiding his hand. With respect, the fire throwers made a place for him by the fire.

The next day, he and the other men were greeted by the maidens of the village as heroes. One named Maile walked shyly beside Kimo and slipped her hand into his. When they reached his father's house, he found both his parents very sick and close to death. He knew worrying about him and his foolishness had aged them.

"From now on," he said, "I will make you proud. I will take care of you until you die as you have cared for me since birth." And he did as he had promised.

Because of his strength and clearness of mind and eye, Kimo, from that day forward was honored as a wise man. To this day on the small, round island in the middle of the sea, the wind roars up the river protecting the bone cave of the sorcerer. And if you wish to find this spot, let your eye follow the cliffs that border the river until you see the dancing Tiki cave.

"She planted a picture of this new island in the sea bird's eye and sent him off to the Earth Mother."

X

How The Earth Mother Came To The Small Round Island Or How The Islands Were Made

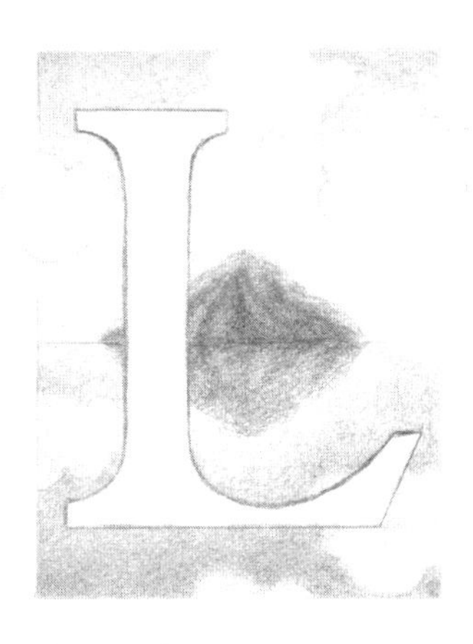

ONG AGO WHEN THE EARTH WAS NEW, Pele, the Goddess of the Volcano, dampened her fire and came to the center of the great blue sea to rest. For seven days and seven nights she lay quietly beneath the ocean floor. On the eighth day she arose refreshed.

She asked Father Sea how she could repay his kindness in protecting her rest. He replied that he longed to see the Earth Mother, but for many years had not found her along the coast where they used to meet.

"She labors in the center of the wide land," Pele said, "where the mountains are newborn and still barren and gray. But if that is your wish, I will try to grant it. I'll stoke my fire and heave it upward here at your center. Maybe I can create a spot so perfect it will tempt her to come. And one so small you will be able to see and touch her wherever she works."

Pele heaved her flames and lava through the sea floor until a small island was born. When it surfaced she called for a sea bird and planted a picture of the island in its eye. Then she sent it to the Earth Mother with a message to come. But the Earth Mother refused, saying her labors were needed where she was. Pele tried again and again, but each time the Earth Mother refused.

Pele underestimated the great depth of the sea's center. The islands she created formed giant sea mountains, but barely broke the surface of the ocean. In high seas many were washed over by waves and disappeared. Father Sea thanked Pele for her hard work, and said he understood how difficult a task she had undertaken.

"I do not give up so easily," Pele replied. "I will rest again. And as I rest, I will gather all my power toward creating a place more beautiful than any other in all the world. I will make an island where the Earth Mother's toil will not mean years of hard work, but moments of sweet joy."

Again Pele banked her fire and rested. On the eighth day she sent a mighty blaze filled with lava through the sea floor, beginning the birth struggle anew. Each day her island grew taller and taller. And each night, Pele inspected her creation for flaws. For this island she intended to be perfect in every way.

The work went slowly. After two hundred days, she sent for the sea bird. She planted a picture of this new island in the sea bird's eye and sent him off to the Earth Mother. Then she and Father Sea waited and waited.

When the sea bird finally returned, he carried the Earth Mother with him. Father Sea and Pele rejoiced. In the morning the Earth Mother inspected Pele's work.

"Pele, it is perfect," she said. "I will make this gift you have given me sparkle as if a cluster of jewels had been gathered together in the middle of the sea."

To start her labors the Earth Mother called all the birds of the sea to the bare island. To each she gave instructions about what seeds they should fetch from which far-off lands.

As she waited for the birds return, she visited with Father Sea and asked him to create clouds to hug the mountain top so that rain would nourish the seeds the birds brought. The two spoke to the sun, promising it a place of beauty on which to shine and give warmth.

"I will provide my radiance if you can convince Father Sea to control his clouds," the sun said.

"It is agreed," rumbled Father Sea.

And last, the Earth Mother asked Father Sea to order his waves to pound the lava that covered the island each day so that the low areas would be receptive to planting and the shore line would have fine white sand. He joyfully agreed.

Soon the sea birds returned from the four corners of the earth, bringing with them seeds from the world's most beautiful flowers and trees. The Earth Mother thanked the birds and gave them a shelf along the coast of the land where they could rest protected from the wind.

For one hundred days Pele, The Earth Mother, Father Sea, the sun and the rain clouds worked together without resting. Even the moon, delighted by the beauty below, stayed full each night to enjoy it. When all was completed, the Earth Mother declared this small, round island in the middle of the sea the most beautiful spot on all the earth.

She was so pleased, she declared, "I will make this place my home."

Father Sea and Pele rejoiced. For seven days and seven nights all who had worked in its creation feasted and played.

But soon Pele grew restless. Her fire rumbled and flared. One day she decided to take her fire to the south and make yet another island, one even grander. This island would have great mountain ranges and wide, calm bays.

After Pele left, the Earth Mother lay down on a foothill of the small, round island to rest. Father Sea, grateful that she had come and ended his loneliness, stood guard over her as she slept, but soon Pele called for his help. Reluctant to leave the Earth Mother unguarded, Father Sea placed a great white shark at her side.

When the island to the south was completed, Pele and Father Sea woke the Earth Mother. And the three labored to create another place of great beauty. But when they were finished, the Earth Mother wanted to return to her small, round island. Pele asked her why she preferred that small island to the larger one just completed. The Earth Mother said only that the new island was much too grand for her. She envisioned that it would one day be a place of great wealth and much too busy and noisy for her.

After the Earth Mother left, Pele and Father Sea went still further south and created yet another island. This one had not only two great mountains upon it, but also small sister islands to embrace it. And on these islands Pele persuaded the sun to shine even more intensely. When they called for her, the Earth Mother came and performed her duties, but this sun-filled island could not tempt her from the gardens of her resting place.

"It is too hot, too clear," she said. "There is no mystery here."

"But even though the Earth Mother had clearly chosen, Pele could not contain her restless quest. This time she went even further south and created an island with five spectacular mountains. Each time she and Father Sea completed a mountain, the Earth Mother would come to create the land that surrounded it. But always at the end, the Earth Mother would return to her beloved island to the north.

And so it goes even to this day. As Pele and Father Sea work on the fifth mountain of that big island in the south, the Earth Mother rests on the small, round island in the middle of the sea. Look up as you travel north along its beaches. There you will see the Earth Mother lying on her foothill, her head tilted back, her hair flowing down over the edge. And beside her, stern and erect, looms the great shark sent to guard her as she sleeps.

ABOUT THE AUTHOR

Joy Jobson is a writer and psychologist who lives on the small, almost round island of Kauai in the Hawaiian islands. She and her husband, Jim Madison, moved there from Eastern Pennsylvania in 1986.

The decision to move was impulsive. After only twenty minutes on the island for vacation, Joy knew she wanted to live there for the rest of her life. At the time she didn't know why Kauai attracted her so or why it was important to leave what had been a very satisfying life in Pennsylvania, but once Jim agreed she never wavered from that decision or had any second thoughts about it. When friends and family asked why, Joy said, "We want to experience ourselves in a different environment and culture to learn and grow." Now she knows also that coming to Kauai was part of a spiritual quest for both of them.

To earn her living, Joy has written for magazines and newspapers on the island, but found factual writing not nearly as much fun as writing fiction. So now she counsels private clients and residents in a drug and alcohol treatment center near her home in Kapaa. One of the reasons she loves working in the addiction field is that it combines psychology, philosophy and spiritual understanding, just as storytelling does. "Stories show a way to solve *a* problem, not *the* way."

To her fourteen grandchildren to whom this book is dedicated, Joy is Grammy Joy. As with so many grandparents, she's found being a grandparent much more fun than being a parent. "Parenthood carried all the burdens of teaching six children about responsibility and duty in life, while being a grandmother only requires enjoying them as they are."

Besides playing with grandchildren, Joy's favorite pastimes are reading, writing, riding waves, playing classical and folk guitar and group singing with friends and in the Kauai Chorale.

ABOUT THE ARTIST

Jean Inaba is a young and successful fine artist who lives on Kauai with her husband, Randy Doi.

Jean Inaba feels that the personalities of artists are reflected in their work, whether they intend it or not. She sees her work as reflecting her heritage and experience as an American of Japanese descent. Many of her paintings and drawings blend the patterns and images of traditional Japan with a more modern feeling of design and abstraction as well as the intense tropical colors of Hawaii. She stylizes her paintings to create an "amalgam of who I am and the influences in my life."

Living in Hawaii has changed Jean's art, not just in color but also in attitude. Her work used to be much darker--sometimes sad or angry. The colors of the island, the gentle environment and her personal growth on Kauai have brought a new peaceful influence to her paintings. Her images reflect this new calm. The figures have trust and hope, they celebrate life and imagination.

Jean was selected as illustrator for *Tales from a Small, Round Island* on the recommendation of a famous and much loved

Kauai artist and poet, Reuben Tam. He felt her skill, composition and vision would add an extra dimension to the stories, would help children enter the world of the story. Jean enjoyed finding the right image for each story. The drawings and water color cover painting for the book were done to fit the dimensions of the book design, a much smaller space than most of her fine art.